Title: His Secret Life
Subtitle: Werewolf Shifter Romance Short Story
Author: Carly Hammer

From the Publisher:
Thank you for purchasing this book.

Table of Contents

Title Page..1

Copyright Page 2

His Secret Life 4

Description...4

Chapter 1 5

Chapter 2...11

Chapter 3...15

Chapter 4.. 19

Chapter 5.. 22

Chapter 6.. 27

Chapter 7..32

Chapter 8..36

Chapter 9..40

His Secret Life
Description

While walking through a dark alley, Casey gets an unsettling feeling, which she dismisses until a disgruntled admirer confronts her. Luckily, she is rescued by a stranger with unforgettable eyes.

Two weeks later, she accepts a job as a night shift receptionist at a motel, but on her first day, she makes a terrible mistake. This mistake reveals a scary secret that Casey is threatened with keeping. She is not so easily swayed, though, especially after identifying her rescuer.

Determined to repay the favor, Casey aids Kenneth, her new boss, and diligently nurses him back to health. This leads to a romantic revelation and a passionate night of lovemaking. But drama follows the couple the following night when Kenneth's former clan leader takes them. There, Kenneth challenges Levi in a match which he heroically wins, earning them their freedom, but this victory also comes with a surprising position.

Chapter 1

"I'm almost there," Casey spoke through her cellular phone as her footsteps echoed through the alley, cutting through the stillness of the night.

The streets were mostly empty now, but hours before, it was bustling with shopping tourists. However, as soon as the sun went down, they fled to their accommodations, leaving the streets to the locals looking for a night of fun.

"I'm going through the alley now. See you in a bit," she told the person on the other end of the phone before ending the call.

Casey walked briskly through the small space, diverting the garbage thrown out by the store owners. The alley was dark, with limited lights at the ends joining the main streets.

As she passed the cluster of cardboard boxes, she stopped and eyed the area behind her where she had just come through. Casey couldn't help having the feeling she was being watched. It was a tingling sensation that created a queasiness in her stomach and put her on edge.

Though she saw no one, the feeling remained, tying her stomach in knots.

Casey shook her head and continued on her path, speeding up her pace to the bar. She had been stressing about not finding a job recently. Maybe it was playing on her mind. Nevertheless, she was relieved when she approached the building with loitering couples and loud music emanating from the inside.

"Casey. Casey. Over here."

Casey scanned the room for where her friend was calling and found her at the far corner with her hand waving wildly in the air. Lil was dressed in a long-sleeved top with extremely short denim shorts. She paired this with black thigh-high boots and flashy accessories that matched her personality. When Casey met Lil, she was a brunette, but since then had become a blonde and now a fiery redhead.

Usually the center of attention, Lil was accustomed to getting her way and sometimes took the privileged act too far. Nevertheless, Casey loved her. She was the first friend Casey met when she moved five years ago, and since then, they had become inseparable.

"What's up, Lil," Casey greeted her friend, taking the seat beside her.

Next to Lil, Casey's outfit was considered boring. She wore dark blue jeans distressed at the knees and a sleeveless top. On her feet were dark brown strapped heeled sandals that matched her side bag with the long strap. Her makeup was kept natural and the only jewelry she wore was a circular gold stud.

Casey wrapped her blonde hair in a ponytail on top of her head and folded it at the ends. During the day she hide behind dark sunglasses but as darkness rolled in, she tucked them into her bag.

"What took you so long?" Lil took one of the shots and placed it in front of Casey.

"My interview went a little long," Cassey told her, breathing out hard. "The manager wanted to know every detail of my life."

"So you got it then," Lil's eyes opened wide, and she sat at the edge of the chair with expectation.

Casey shook her head and wrapped her hand around the glass. "No. He said I wasn't what he was looking for."

Lil released a series of obscenities, followed by speculations about the manager's choice in women.

"Don't worry, Casey," she said when she calmed down. "You'll find something soon."

Casey kept her head down and let her friend's reassuring words float past her.

"Oh, I'll be right back," Lil stood suddenly. "I had a few drinks before you came and I think they're ready to come out." Lil squeezed her thighs together and disappeared into the crowd in the washroom's direction.

Left alone to reflect on her failed interview, Casey tossed her head back and gulped down the shot. However, a deep voice almost caused her to choke.

"Mind if I join you?" The man that spoke wore a light blue shirt and dark trousers. He was big, but not quite muscular. and sported a rugged beard.

Casey pointed in the direction Lil had disappeared. "I already have company. She'll be back any minute."

"I saw that friend of yours," the man said. "She can't satisfy you the way I can."

Casey jerked her head back at the man's shocking comment. "Is this your idea of picking up women?" she asked.

The man kept his body upright, holding her gaze. "I'm simply stating the facts."

Casey was usually polite and composed, and it took more than a little forwardness to get her rattled. She leaned back in the seat. "Well, thanks for the information, but I don't need satisfying. I'm pretty content."

The man narrowed his eyes and adopted a rigid posture. "Why don't you think it over?" he asked in a low, rumbling tone. "You might regret it."

Casey smiled then. Her forehead was wrinkled. "I assure you I won't."

"If you say so," he retorted before walking away.

Long after the man left, Casey still couldn't shake that eerie feeling that lingered around their conversation. The glint in his eyes also rattled her insides.

"Are you ready for a fun night?" the words came from behind and Casey squinted at her friend's voice. "See. This is exactly what I'm talking about," Lil said as she reclaimed her seat. "You need to drink, relax, and have fun."

That was exactly what the women did, but at the end of the night, Lil was the one completely intoxicated. Casey called her friend a cab, told the driver her address, and took the driver's information. Then she staggered lower down the street to get a bus. It was already late but being jobless did not allow Casey such luxuries as to hire two taxis in one night. Lil's cab fare alone had sent her night's budget over the edge, so she decided that no matter the time, she would wait for the bus.

Casey was the only one around when she felt it again. The same eerie feeling that caused the tiny hairs on her hand to become erect. It was a feeling that unsettled her at her core, so she pushed herself off the bus stop bench and track a route to the bar she had left when a man suddenly intercepted her path, gazing at her with malice.

Casey altered her direction to walk around him, but the man made it impossible for her to pass. She took a step back and stared up at his face instead, recognizing his twisted lip immediately.

"Can you please get out of my way?" Casey pushed out her chest and held her chin high. She was trying hard not to show her fear.

"Where's your friend now?" The man growled before looking around. "Seems like she abandoned you."

"She did not abandon me. She just went around the corner for something." Casey gripped the strap of her bag tighter.

The man opened his eyes wide and tilted his chin. "Is that right? Cause I could have sworn it was her I saw getting into that sedan earlier."

Casey took a step back then, her heart speeding at an alarming rate.

"You know what I think," the man decreased the distance between them. "I think you're all alone."

He reached out to her and caught her shoulder as Casey screamed and tried to free herself.

She was still tugging in his arms when a booming voice caused both of them to turn sharply.

"Let her go." The stranger approached them slowly with his hand in his pocket. He stood with his body tall, not that he needed any extra height. He was easily a foot taller than Casey.

She eyed him from head to toe. Taking in his curly dark brown hair and uniquely green eyes. This man's face was covered in facial hair, giving him a rugged but sexy look. Though the situation was not suited for it, Casey felt the shudders in her loins and turned her head.

"Mind your business, man, and you won't get hurt." Casey's attacker was still holding on to her.

The handsome stranger that was awakening her sensitivity stopped in front of them. "If you walk away now, maybe I'll allow you to keep your legs."

Casey's attacker gave the stranger a hateful glare and cackled before his expression suddenly changed. His mouth fell open and at the same time, his eyes widened and his grip loosened.

"What the hell are you?" were his last words before he turned and bolted out of sight. Casey kept her eyes on him until he disappeared.

"You shouldn't walk the streets alone at this hour." She turned around to take in the stranger's pronounced jawline. Being this close to him now was almost intoxicating.

Casey swallowed hard. "Thank you," she said, but the man was already walking away.

Chapter 2

Casey lifted her feet high to cross the threshold lined with buckets to catch the leaking water. The lobby of the motel was small, but at least it wasn't completely dilapidated, like some of the others she had been to.

"Hello." Casey walked up to the man at the front desk to get his attention. Though her arrival was not quite, the man didn't bother to raise his head from the newspaper. "I have an interview with Mr. Lessey."

The man turned around then and took in her appearance. She was wearing dark blue jeans with a pink t-shirt and sneakers. Her makeup was light and her hair was pulled into a low ponytail. Casey believed she had dressed appropriately for the interview but as beady eyes scanned her, doubts filled her head.

Casey clutched the strap of her bag. "Do you know where I can find him?"

"That would be me," the man said, folding his newspaper and swinging himself around on the chair. "Did you bring your resume?"

"Yes, I did." Casey dug into her bag and produced the white envelope, offering it to her interviewer.

The man scanned the pages of the document while Casey shifted from one foot to another. "Are you comfortable working night shifts?"

Casey took in a breath and held it. The truth was that she was not. She hated staying up all night, but if she wanted to keep her apartment, she needed a job as soon as possible.

"Yes, I am," Casey lied and fisted her hand at her back in hopes that her interviewer would not notice the twitching of her jaw.

The man looked up from the documents she handed him. "Can you start immediately?"

Casey swallowed hard as a small smile curled her lips. "Sure. That is not a problem."

"One last thing. You would also be expected to perform some personal assistant duties to the owner. He has certain... requests to be done every twenty-nine to thirty days. It is very important that you follow these instructions exactly." The man spoke with intense eyes, willing her to acknowledge the seriousness of his words.

Casey nodded in acknowledgment. "What do I have to do?"

The man lowered his eyes. "Nothing difficult. Starting tonight, at seven, lock his room from the outside and whatever you do, do not go in."

Casey's eyelashes fluttered rapidly, but the rest of her body remained unfazed. She wanted to enquire about the strange task but had a feeling she wouldn't get an answer even if she did, so she kept her questions to herself. "Understood."

"Great," the man said, scooped up his newspaper, and made his way out of the receptionist area. "Everything else is straightforward. When someone comes in, you take their money and give them a key. The rates of the rooms are on the counter. You also have to record everything in the notebook."

Casey scanned the area, her eyes landing on the laminated sheet taped to the countertop. "Ok."

Before the man left the building, he said. "I will be back to relieve you in the morning. Don't forget to lock the door."

"I won't," Casey said, entering the small receptionist's area.

Casey scanned her surroundings. Keys lined the wall, each one attached to a numbered tag. Some slots were missing a key and Casey assumed they were the rooms that were already filled.

She flipped open the notebook to the last used page. Lines were drawn from top to bottom to create columns, each one requiring different information. Then she snapped the book closed and dropped herself onto the chair, breathing out hard.

"It's not the best situation," she said, noting the faded paint on the walls. "But it will do for now."

Sighing, she took out her phone and stored her bag in the cupboard below. Then she texted her best friend informing her of her job status. Lil didn't respond, so Casey stuffed her headphones in her ear and turned on the music. No one entered the building after her and before long she was consumed by the musical tracks of Avril Lavigne.

It was the rumbling of her stomach that snapped Casey out of her pop-rock trace as her eyes went to the clock on the wall. Her head jerked back immediately and her eyes widened as she discovered her first on-the-job mistake. Without haste, Casey bolted from her seat and dashed towards the door that Mr. Lessey had pointed to when speaking of the owner. She scurried down the hallway, almost tripping on her feet, and collided with the door, knocking her shoulder slightly.

Casey moaned and rubbed the tender area before reaching for the two rim locks and the three-barrel bolts attached to the door. It was then that she heard it. Low grunting sounds much like her own, but more intense.

Her body froze as she recalled Mr. Lessey's instructions. "Do not go in." He gave her that warning for a reason, but how could she ignore the pained sounds coming from the inside? What if the owner of the motel was hurt and in need of assistance? She couldn't just stand outside, knowing that she might be able to do something to help. So instead of following instructions on her first day of work, Casey pushed open the metal door and barged into the room, but the sight that greeted her was far from what she expected.

Standing in the middle of the sitting room was a man, only he didn't quite look like a man. His ears were erect, but it was not as pronounced as the nose that extended from his face. The man's fingers were replaced with claws and his body was covered with overgrown hair. Casey stood frozen, her heart beating rapidly and eyes widened as the man's canine teeth extended beyond what was considered normal.

A gasp escaped her then, and it seemed to capture the man's attention. He turned towards her, eyes a brilliant yellow, and roared in a half animalistic voice. "Get out of here now."

Though her mind was still in a daze, her body sprang back into action then, as she turned abruptly and scampered out. Casey slammed the door shut behind her, locking it with shaky hands and a rapid breath. Then she slowly backed away, not willing to accept what she had seen.

Chapter 3

Fragments of the night occupied Casey's thoughts throughout the following day. She couldn't quite comprehend what she saw, but she knew it wasn't natural and it definitely wasn't something she should have seen.

"How am I supposed to go to that place again?" Casey spoke to herself in the mirror as she dressed for her shift. She felt as if her mind was asleep and her body was simply going through the motions.

Great! At least this way she would be detached from whatever happened on her shift.

Casey kept that mentality as she walked into the lobby, her eyes wondering wildly at the paintings on the wall.

"What the hell did you do last night?" Mr. Lessey caused the weight of her feet to halt all their movement.

"What do you mean?" Casey stammered while clutching her bag. She knew exactly what she did, enter the owner's room, yet she pretended to be clueless. Maybe if she denied it, she wouldn't be forced to recall the frightful sight that prevented her from closing her eyes the entire day.

"I don't know what you did, but he's pissed." The 'he,' Mr. Lessey was referring to, was obviously the owner of the motel. "He asked me to send you to his apartment the moment you came in today."

Casey swallowed hard, her voice shaky. "He wants me to go in there?" She pointed to the room, numbered 101.

"That's what I said, didn't I? Just make it quick and return to your post as soon as possible. I'm leaving as soon as the clock strikes seven." Mr. Lessey turned away from her then, blocking his face with the day's newspaper, which signified the end of their conversation.

Casey sighed, her stomach in turmoil and her face ashen.

"The longer you wait, the more pissed he's going to become. My advice is to just get it over with." The man spoke without looking away from the newspaper.

Casey took a deep breath and willed her feet down the corridor, where she knocked on the door, she had scampered out of just the night before. Her hand was shaking, but it seemed to freeze when the deep masculine voice on the other side of the door said, "Come in."

With wavering steps, she entered the apartment, surprised by what she saw. The night before, she was too taken aback to pay attention to anything but the morphing figure in the middle of the room, a room which she now appreciated for its intricate design.

Casey was expecting a bachelor pad, maybe a lazy boy couch, and a large screen television but as she looked around then, she couldn't even spot the entertainment electronic. There was, however, a large bookshelf laden with the reading materials. Next to it was a single couch with a side table to its right. On that table was a lamp and three hardcover books. It was close to the window with burglar-proof bars sporting clusters of indentations. Besides the single couch, there were two others, both covered with sheets.

"Have a seat." Casey dropped into the closest couch as soon as she heard the deep rumbling. She had almost forgotten her situation until her boss spoke. His body turned away from her to stare at an open window.

"Do you know who I am?" Her boss kept his tone indifferent and his posture relaxed.

"You're the owner of this motel. Kenneth." Casey kept her hands in her lap, nervously entwining her fingers together.

"Yes, I am," the man said, his hand in his pocket. "And as your boss, I constructed rules. Rules that you broke on your first night here."

Casey kept her head low but said nothing. She was waiting for the wrath she was certain would follow.

"The rules were simple." Kenneth raked his hand through his curly, dark brown hair. "Lock the door and do not enter under any circumstances."

"I heard a noise, and I thought you might have been in trouble." Casey allowed her voice to flow across the room, but she was unsure if it reached his ears.

"What did you see?" The man's shoulder was stiffening with tension.

"I... I didn't see anything," Casey said, her voice rattling.

Kenneth obviously didn't believe her since his voice became harsh, his swift movement as he turned around startling Casey. "If you tell anyone what you saw here last night, I will come after you. Do you understand me?"

Casey's eyes were closed, but she nodded her response.

"Open your eyes and answer me with words. I need to make sure you understand me and do as I say this time," came the harsh command.

Her eyes opened then to unique green ones. Casey had seen eyes like that only two weeks ago when a stranger saved her from a man outside the bar.

Those eyes weren't hostile. They weren't the eyes of someone with the slightest aggressiveness, but they were defensive. Casey held Kenneth's gaze and for a moment, they both said nothing as the tension left her body, washing her with relief.

"It was you, wasn't it?" Her legs suddenly gained strength, and she stood, inches away from the man who just threatened her. "It was you who saved me close to the bar that night."

Kenneth swallowed hard and turned away from her, his hands fidgeting. "I don't know what you're talking about."

It was an obvious lie.

"You stopped that guy from harassing me two weeks ago," she said in a low, amusing tone.

Kenneth's words were harsh now, but Casey didn't believe he intended to hurt her at all. He was just putting on an act so that she wouldn't tell others about what she saw.

Though Casey wasn't even sure of what happened the night before, she wouldn't tell anyone. How could she endanger someone who had saved her?

"You risked your life to save me that night, but I never got a chance to thank you. So, I am thanking you now." Casey turned to leave, but before she did, she left Kenneth with reassuring words. "And you don't have to worry. I wouldn't say anything to anyone about what I saw here last night."

Chapter 4

Casey returned to the receptionist's desk, but every so often her eyes darted to the door to Kenneth's apartment. She had called his bluff, and he was completely stunned, reassuring her she was right. Kenneth never intended to harm her, only scare her in keeping his secret. A secret she had no intention of revealing.

The door opened, signaling the first guest of the night, but it wasn't the crowd Casey was expecting. The night before occupants of the motel room was mainly coupled. Couples of all sorts, but couples. But these first guest was a group of well-built men. Three followed the lead of a bald, rugged man and even dusted the drops of rain from his jacket as he entered.

Casey followed them with narrowed eyes until they stopped at her desk. The bald one pierced her with his eyes, his jaw twitching, but it wasn't him that spoke. "We are here to see Kenneth."

She looked from one to the other, then rested on the leader. These were definitely not guests; she was certain of it. And even more certain, they would cause nothing but trouble.

"Is he expecting you?" She stood erect and kept her voice steady, unwilling to show these men the slightest hint she was unsure of herself. Her boss had defended her and she would do her best to repay the favor.

"We don't need an appointment," minion number one said. "Just point us in the right direction."

Casey turned her gaze from the subordinate to the leader. She lifted her chin and stood tall. "I'm sorry I can't do that. Why don't you give me your names and I will check if he can see you?"

"Why you little..." the minion began, but the rising of the boss' hand quickly cut him off.

"You must not know who I am, but I can assure you, I am not someone who you want to mess with. I can make your entire life vanish with just a single bite." The bald man peeled back his lip to reveal extended canines.

Casey gasp. Her hand flew up to her chest, trying to calm her racing heart. These men were not completely human in the same way her boss wasn't.

"What do you think you're doing?"

Casey whipped her head around at the sound of a familiar voice. Her boss was standing at his doorway, his hand folded into a fist with furious eyes directed at her. "How dare you refuse my guests?"

"I'm sorry but..." Casey dropped her hand, her breathing somewhat regulating in Kenneth's presence.

"No buts. In fact, why don't you leave for the rest of the night and we will discuss this in the morning?"

Casey's face fell and her legs were weakening. "But I just started my shift."

"And I just ended it," Kenneth said with some finality. "Now leave before I send you home permanently." Then to his guest, he said. "I am sorry about my receptionist. She is new. Come this way and we will talk."

As the men followed Kenneth into his apartment, Casey didn't miss the smirk that stretched across the bald man's face. "Count yourself lucky," he said and disappeared into the apartment.

Releasing a heavy sigh, Casey allowed her body to drop on the chair as her eyes flickered from her boss' door to where her bag rested in the cupboard. She was instructed to leave, but her intuition urged her to stay. Those men were brimming with hostility and it gave her an uneasiness in her stomach. So Casey lingered around.

She was brainstorming for excuses why she disobeyed jet another instruction, why she remained at her post, when the first set of banging caused her to jump in her seat. It was followed by a series of shattering glass and scuffling. When something heavy hit her boss' door, Casey squealed and clutched to the edge of her desk. The need to enter the apartment was strong, but her legs wouldn't dare take her there. They suffered from a sudden loss of energy.

When the door opened, it was the four men who emerged, their faces bright with laughter. The bald one kept his eyes on her and just before he exited the building, he sent her a kiss and licked his lips. Casey stared at him, wide mouth and slightly shivering. She was only able to move several seconds after the men disappeared.

Only then she was able to rush into the completely ramshackle room. Broken glass from the lamp lay at her feet, next to shards of furniture. Casey took her time navigating through the mess. Four evenly long strokes tore the cushions for the couch, revealing the foam inside. Those two were scattered around the room now, housing a fist-size hole in the wall.

"Kenneth?" Casey called with a choked voice, but it was met with no response. Her heart rate quickened in fear that something had happened to him. The next time she screamed his name, there was an urgency in her voice and she spun around wide, her eyes fluttering to all the corners of the room.

Finally, she noticed a motionless body barely recognizable.

Chapter 5

Casey scampered to the unconscious man, kneeling to roll him over, better assessing his condition.

"Kenneth," she nudged gently. When he didn't respond, he called again in a louder voice, her shakes becoming more frantic.

Kenneth's face was busted, and there was a heavy flow of blood coming from his head. His hand was twisted backward in an unnatural way, certainly broken.

Casey patted her pockets and when her hand rested on her phone, she took it out and dialed a number. "Please don't be dead," she urged as her eyes filled with moisture.

While waiting for the person on the other end of the line to pick up, Casey squeezed her eyelids shut and pressed her free hand to her forehead. There was a lot of tension there and the back of her head was beginning to pain.

"Put down the phone." Casey's eyes flew open to the sound of the weakened voice.

Releasing a held breath, she said, "Don't worry. I'm getting you help." She felt as if a heavy load had been taken off her shoulders.

"No, don't." Kenneth struggled to sit up, sending him into a coughing fit.

Casey kept her gaze on him even as the emergency personnel called to her on the line. Kenneth was seriously hurt, and she didn't understand why he didn't want to go to the hospital. If she didn't get him help, she was certain he would die.

"Please Casey, put down the phone." Kenneth's hand rested on her wrist, causing a tingling and warm sensation.

Casey couldn't help but stare into Kenneth's pleading eyes as she spoke through the phone. "Never mind, he woke up," she said right before she cut off the phone. To him, she said, "I don't know why you didn't want me to call the ambulance, but I trust you."

Kenneth's eyes closed then, and his body seemed to relax. "Can you help me to the couch?"

Casey nodded and angled her hand to give support to Kenneth as he pulled his body upward. His movements were slow, and he moaned and clung to his ribs with every step. When Casey lowered him to the hard surface, he grimaced and the wound at his ribs flowed heavier.

"Tell me what you need," Casey urged as her heart ached from watching him in so much agony.

Kenneth groaned and closed his eyes as he leaned back on the couch. His jaw was tight and there were creases on his forehead. "A washcloth and time."

Casey didn't know about time, but a washcloth she could handle. She rushed into the back and pulled one from the towel rack in the bathroom. When she returned, Kenneth's hand was soaked in blood. Casey paused before rushing to him, applying the cloth to his wound. She pressed hard, using her full force until the heavy flow of blood trickled away. Casey sighed then, as the tension in her shoulders relaxed, though the tightness in her chest did not disappear.

"You have to help me with my arm."

Casey's eyes grew wide as she struggled to decipher her boss' words. "What?"

"My hand is broken. Help me pop it back so that it could heal." Kenneth's voice was a little stronger. "I heal fast, so we need to do it now."

Casey remained in her stooped position. "I can't."

"Yes, you can. Just hold it and pop it back in. Don't worry, I won't feel a thing," Kenneth reassured her, and she slowly took a position to better allow her to complete her task.

When Casey pulled on Kenneth's arm, there was a loud popping sound and he screamed and grind his teeth.

"I thought you said it wouldn't hurt." Casey's voice was high-pitched as she backed away.

Kenneth looked at her. "Would you have done it if I said it would be excruciating?"

He was right, of course. If she knew the extent of his pain, she could have never force herself to reconstruct his hand. Sighing, she lowered her head and willed herself to return to his side. "What do I do now?"

"Now you give me time," Kenneth said, and leaned his head back and closed his eyes. His body became still and Casey hoped he was only sleeping.

With Kenneth incapacitated, Casey took the opportunity to tend to his wounds. Finding scissors was time-consuming, but eventually, she retrieved one from the top draw in his bathroom. Then she used it to cut his shirt off, exposing his broad chest, which sent shivers throughout her body. Shivers that were followed by a loud gasp.

Casey blocked her mouth with her hand, both from shock and to stop herself from screaming. She couldn't believe her eyes, even as she lowered her head to get a closer look at Kenneth's skin pulling together and closing the wound. "What are you?" she whispered, knowing that he could not hear her.

Despite her curiosity and confusion, she silently cleaned Kenneth's wounds, which were looking less severe.

Then she went to the kitchen, busying herself. When Kenneth wake, he would need sustenance to help him heal.

She found a parcel of chicken and some vegetables and used it to create a healthy soup. Casey was pouring it into a bowl when she heard him stir.

"You're awake?" Casey said as she brought the bowl with the hot broth to his side. "I made soup for you," she said as Kenneth pushed himself into a seated position. When he took the bowl from her, he used the hand which had been twisted backward earlier. Casey paused and took a few seconds before relinquishing the bowl.

"Careful. It's hot," she warned as Kenneth took the bowl with his bare hands. Her eyes widened then. Even with mittens on, she still felt the heat from the soup, yet Kenneth held it with ease.

He must have noticed her loose jaw because he said, "Don't worry. I don't burn easily." He took one spoonful and rest the bowl on the table. "Aren't you going to ask?"

Casey tilted her head. "What?"

He held her gaze. "Usually, it's the first thing people want to know. Aren't you curious about what you saw the other night and how I'm healing so quickly?"

Casey kept her head low and toyed with her fingers. "I am," she said softly. "But I thought it might be rude to ask."

Her response caused laughter to erupt from Kenneth. "I knew since I first saw you, you were different." Then he leaned back on the couch, folded his arms, and asked with a raised eyebrow. "Why are you helping me? After everything you've observed. Why do you stay? Why did you even come to work today?"

Casey shrugged. "I don't know. I guess I knew you would not hurt me. I can sense that you are a good person."

"You are a brave one, Casey. I like that," Kenneth said, a smile suddenly growing on his face. He reached forward, took the bowl, and spoke in between bites. "As you realize, I'm not entirely human. I'm part human, part wolf. What some would call a werewolf."

Suddenly, it made sense. The night before had been a full moon and if the legends were true, that would incite an involuntary transformation where the wolf could not control himself.

"How long have you been this way?" Casey wasn't sure she should ask, but she did anyway. She somehow felt at ease with Kenneth.

"I was born this way. My parents were both werewolves, but some of us are transformed."

Then her thoughts went back to the men from earlier. "Were those guys werewolves, too?"

Kenneth nodded. "Levi is the leader of the pack. A pack that I no longer want to be in."

Casey tilted her head, and her voice softened. "Is that why they did this to you?"

Kenneth didn't have to respond. His silence was her answer. "I want you to promise me you wouldn't engage in any more confrontation with those men."

"Well, technically, they-" Casey started, but Kenneth cut her off.

"Casey, they are dangerous. I want you to promise me you would stay away." Kenneth's nose flared, and he willed her with his eyes. Suddenly she realized why he directed anger towards her and why he abruptly dismissed her before. Kenneth knew what those men were capable of, and he was trying to protect.

"I will," she said, intending to keep this promise.

Chapter 6

When Casey returned home early the next morning, she dropped herself on the couch and fell asleep, cuddled into a ball. The day had been eventful, and she was exhausted, physically and mentally.

Casey spent her entire day lounging around in the apartment, her thoughts straying to Kenneth's bare chest and toned abs. It felt wrong to ogle at him when he was unconscious, but she couldn't help it. Being that close to his half-naked body was torturous.

That evening, Casey dressed with care. Giving her makeup a little more attention than usual. She wore a long-sleeve patterned dress that matched the army green bootie perfectly. Casey didn't want to appear as if she was trying too hard, so she kept her accessories simple, settling for a pearl stud. Her hair was placed into a half-up, half-down style with a few loose strands at the front. The outfit was more elaborate and feminine than what she usually wore for a night shift, but with Kenneth around, her femineity had been awoken.

Kenneth emerged through the main entrance, looking like nothing had happened the previous night after Casey had taken over from Mr. Lessey. He was dressed in jeans and a t-shirt which advertised his toned body. Casey swallowed hard and allowed her feet to give way as her body dropped into the chair at her station.

Kenneth didn't seem to notice the effect he had on her. "Casey," he called, stopping at her desk. "Do you have time after your shift? I would like to take you somewhere."

Casey held back her excitement, shielding her enthusiasm with a composed demeanor. "Sure. I have time. Where do you want to go?"

"It's a surprise," Kenneth said, a one-sided smile framing his lips. "But I guarantee you will like it."

"Ok then," Casey said, pretending to shuffle through papers as Kenneth walked away.

The seconds seemed to drag into each other as Casey waited for the end of her shift. When Mr. Lessey came, her bag was already packed, and she was drumming her fingers against the counter. Kenneth had gone out, instructing her to wait at the front of the building, and this was an instruction she was definitely following.

Kenneth pulled up in a 2015 Toyota Corolla and Casey scampered in without a word. He took her out of the busy city streets to where time seemed to stop, at which point they were the only ones on the road. Casey kept her eyes on the window, mesmerized by the crashing of the waves as it frothed on the white sand. Through the dim light of the receding moon, she was able to appreciate the beauty of the seaside.

Kenneth drove in silence, only stopping when he parked the car on top of a hill overlooking the ocean. "This is my favorite spot," he said, keeping his eyes forward. "I come here sometimes to watch the sunrise."

Casey turned her head in the direction he watched as a flicker of gold highlighted the horizon. The light struck the blue-green waters, giving it the illusion of golden sparkles. "I can see why. This is really beautiful." Casey said nothing after that, taking in the ambiance of their secluded spot.

Long after the sun had fully risen in the sky, Casey spoke again. She didn't want to damper the mood, but she had to know. "Why did you bring me here?" Then she threw up her hands in the air as her question came out unappreciative. "Not that I'm complaining or anything. I just want to know why me. Why share your spot with me?"

Kenneth looked at her, then turned his head away. "I honestly don't know." He breathed out hard. "I just felt a connection to you." He gazed into her eyes then, his jaw twitching. "You are so different from the women I'm used to encountering. I like that."

Different? What did that even mean?

Casey turned away from him as he continued. "You're brave, even in the worst of circumstances. You're smart, beautiful, and funny."

Her cheeks brightened at the sound of his words. "You never give up and you're a good friend, considerate and kind."

It was then her head turned to stare at Kenneth. He only met her three days ago. There was no way he knew all those things about her.

"I was in the club that night," he continued. "The night that pervert attacked you," Kenneth said the words with scorn before his tone became light. "I followed you there."

Casey kept her eyes fixed on him, unsure of how she should interpret his words. "When I saw your applicant picture, it was like I was drawn to you. So I went to your house that day and followed you from there. I'm sorry." Kenneth blew out hard. "I only meant to watch from a distance, but when I saw you in need, I just had to help. I hoped I haven't freaked you out."

Casey shook her head. "Watching your flesh fuse back together didn't scare me off. What makes you think this will?"

The couple held each other's gaze as the space between them minimized. When Kenneth brushed her lips with his, a rush of energy overwhelmed Casey, and she found herself pulling him into her. Her stomach was fluttering and her skin surged with sensitivity.

They clung to each other, Kenneth with his hand wrapped around the small of her back while Casey's was linked behind his neck.

"I feel the same way about you," Casey said when she was finally allowed to breathe. "That sight the other night should have scared me away, but I came back because somehow I knew you were not a threat to me. I knew you wouldn't harm me, and the night before solidified that. I can't stop myself from pulling towards you. I don't want to."

Casey batted her eyelashes, and Kenneth smiled. "Then don't," he said, placing her loose hair behind her ears. "Give into that urge that wants to be with me."

It was Casey who initiated the kiss, pulling Kenneth closer so that her breast pressed against his chest. She moaned into his mouth as her hand went under his shirt, gently stroking his chest.

Kenneth released her to free himself from the material as Casey tugged at the zipper of his jeans. When he was free, she took him in her hand, massaging as his appendage twitched. It didn't take long for him to moisten her hand.

When Casey leaped over the gears to sit on his lap, Kenneth held on to her waist. Then his hand dropped lower and under her dress to caress her thighs. Eventually, his roaming hand slid down to her sensitive area, sliding across the lace of her underwear. Casey held her breath and waited for what was to come.

As Kenneth entered her, her head went backward, and she pushed out her chest. Kenneth's hand went to her rounded mold, and he massaged it as Casey rocked her hips back and forth. Kenneth fit inside her perfectly. It was as if they belonged to each other. He was close to his climax when he felt Casey convulse around his manhood, urging him to follow.

Their orgasm was explosive, wild, and intense, just like their feelings toward each other.

"I never want this feeling to go away," Casey said after she could speak again.

Kenneth smiled and pushed her loose hair behind her ears again. "As long as I'm by your side, it wouldn't."

Chapter 7

The look on Mr. Lessey's face as Kenneth and Casey crossed the lobby to enter Kenneth's apartment together was amusing. The newspaper fell from him with his hand still in the air as he watched them, wide-eyed. Before Kenneth closed the door behind them, Casey noticed him pushing his neck out for a better view.

"I suppose Mr. Lessey is in a state of shock," Kenneth said, turning towards Casey.

Casey had a frown on her face and her eyes were dull. "I supposed coming here was a bad idea."

Kenneth reached out and caressed her shoulders then. "No, it is not. I want you here." Then he placed a kiss on her lips.

The kiss was the start of another intense episode of lovemaking. Casey latched on to Kenneth, pulling him closer as they ravaged each other. Then he unzipped her dress, dropping it to her feet as she kicked the material free.

"Wow," he said, staring at her sultry underwear. It was a purple lace set she had spoiled herself with. "If you wear things like that, I might never make you leave."

Casey smiled and put her hand at her back to unclasp her bra. "What if I wore nothing?" she said, dropping the lacey material to the ground.

"Then you're definitely not leaving." Kenneth pulled her towards him before taking her in his arms and dropping her on the bed. Then he amazed her by tearing this t-shirt and dropping the rags to the side. Casey's eyes widened at the show of masculinity. She was still in awe when Kenneth dropped the rest of his clothing as his manhood sprang free.

He climbed over her then, poking her in the stomach and causing her to giggle.

"Hmm," Kenneth tilted his head. "That is not the sound I want to hear from you."

Casey creased her forehead and pushed up her nose. "What is?"

Kenneth's movement was swift, then. He lowered his body, angling his penis so he slid into Casey's entrance. Casey gasped as she swallowed him. "That is," Kenneth said, displaying a seductive smirk.

Casey grabbed him around the neck and pulled his lips to hers as his thrust caused a tingling sensation in her most sensitive area. With each movement, her sounds became louder, more distinct, until Casey was moaning rather loudly. When she reached her climax, she screamed his name as her body fell backward onto the bed. Kenneth followed her.

"That was amazing," Kenneth said, pulling Casey to him.

She wrapped her feet around him and toyed with the fine hairs on his chest. "Most definitely," she said, with a sparkle in her eye. "But now I'm completely famished."

"Hmm," Kenneth stroked her hair. "Someone made mouthwatering soup for me yesterday. I could warm some up for you?"

Casey pushed herself from the tangled mass of limbs. "Nope. You just lie here and relax. I will take care of it."

Though she intended to make her way to the kitchen, she didn't move at the same time and Kenneth latched on to her arm. "If you don't let me go, we're going to starve to death."

"Then I will die a happy man," he chuckled.

"Not on my watch," Casey said, prying his fingers away, one at a time. When she was free, she sprinted into the kitchen with no clothing. Kenneth followed her about thirty minutes after and by that time Casey had toasted some bread, created a salad, and warmed up the soup. He pulled her in for a kiss before grabbing a bowl.

The couple had almost finished their meal when Casey looked at the mosaic clock and frowned. "It's time for me to take my shift. I suspect Mr. Lessey has already gone."

Kenneth covered her hand with his. "You must be tired. Why don't you go home and rest? I will handle your shift."

He was right. Casey was tired. Not only did she not sleep after her last shift, but she had been doing hard exercise all day.

"Really?" she said, her smile pushing at her cheeks. "You are wonderful."

Kenneth was not beyond being smug. "It's just one of my many traits."

Casey dressed and prepared to leave shortly after that. Her intention was to head home, have a nice long shower, then sleep. Hopefully, until the sun went down again.

She left the apartment first with her eyes partially closed, reminiscing about the day. She hadn't expected to find anyone in the lobby, much less to walk into them.

"I'm so sorry," she said. Backing away from the solid mass, she raised her head to find piercing eyes and a grim expression. It was accompanied by a bald head and fanged teeth.

"Well, look who it is, boys," the leader of the werewolf clan spoke. "I must admit, I was disappointed to not see you behind the desk tonight." He looked past her to where she had emerged from. "But it looks like you got a promotion."

Remembering what she had promised Kenneth, Casey said nothing, kept her head down, and attempted to walk around the man, but he clung to her shoulder. "Don't leave so soon. The fun is just beginning."

"Let me go," she screamed and struggled unsuccessfully in his arms. At the same time, Kenneth burst into the hallway, his eyes raging at the sight that confronted him.

"What are you doing?" he shouted, the veins on his face and neck pronounced. "Let her go."

The bald man smirked, then pushed Casey into the arms of his number one subordinate. "I think you forget your place, Kenneth," he said in a slow, raspy voice. "How dare you tell me what to do?" He made a low sinister growl.

Kenneth lowered his head then but kept his eyes on Casey. "She has nothing to do with this."

The bald man looked back at her. "But she is your weakness." He caressed Casey's cheek. "And having her in my possession means I have control over you."

"You piece of shit," Kenneth said, racing towards the man, but a minion blindsided him and knocked him out.

Chapter 8

Casey screamed as Kenneth fell to the floor, blood flowing from the side of his head. She knew his healing ability was extremely impressive, but what good would it do if he were dead? She struggled free and raced to his side, only to be recaptured. The last thing she remembered before everything went dark was kicking a minion in his most delicate area.

"Casey, can you hear me?" His voice was low, but she knew it well. "Casey, wake up."

Casey groaned and fluttered her eyes open, only to close them again in disbelief.

"Casey, listen to me. I'm going to get you out of here. Do you hear me? I will get you away from all of this."

Casey's head moved slowly as she assessed the situation. She and Kenneth were in an empty room, tied to chairs.

"Where are we?" she asked, still partially dazed.

"We're at the clan's base. Levi plans to make an example of me so no one would dare try to leave the clan again." Kenneth's breath was shallow, and he seemed to be tugging at the bonds on his wrist.

"What's going to happen to us?" Casey's voice was shaky now and some of her words got lost before they reached Kenneth. Her eyes were wide and her lips quivered, giving her the appearance of a child.

"Nothing," Kenneth said firmly, forcing her to look at him. "Because I'm going to get us out of here."

At that time, the door pushed open and the Levi and two of his subordinates entered the room, each sporting a satisfied grin.

"Dammit, Levi." Kenneth roared. "Let us go."

Levi walked slowly towards him. "After I went to all the trouble of summoning the entire clan here. I don't think so."

"We did nothing wrong." Kenneth was still trying to set himself free, but Levi didn't seem concerned.

"You know, in the old days, abandoning your clan was a crime punishable by death." He lowered himself to stare into Kenneth's eyes. "I miss those days. Don't you?" Levi began to pace. "See, you are one of the strongest warrior I have. I had plans to groom you as my second in command. I can't lose you." He looked at Casey, his nose flared. "And definitely not to her."

"I will not fight for you if you harm her." Kenneth was practically screaming.

"I will harm her if you don't," Levi smirked again, this time flashing his elongated canines.

Kenneth remained silent and held his head low. Then suddenly he raised it as if just remembering something. "I challenge you to a duel."

Levi's head whipped around and his voice was hoarse. "What?"

"You heard me." Kenneth kept his voice low and even. "I challenge you, Levi, leader of the clan. If I win, you release us both and never bother us again. And if I lose, I return to the clan and fight for you without resistance."

Levi burst into laughter, his tone amused. "I admit you are a good fighter, Kenneth. But I am the best in this clan. There is no way you can win against me."

"Then you have nothing to worry about," Kenneth blurted.

Levi went quiet for a while, pondering Kenneth's proposition. "Fine then. I look forward to you rejoining the clan."

One of the men released Kenneth then, and he nodded to her before heading for the door. Before Levi left, she told his subordinates. "Bring her. I want her to be there when her boyfriend loses." Then he left.

A minion untied Casey and escorted her to an open room. There was a large crowd around the exterior, but in the middle, Kenneth and Levi, both were preparing themselves mentally for the fight.

Casey didn't know what to expect, but she certainly was not prepared for what she saw. Both men growled and howled as their bodies stressed and morphed out of their human form. Their ears projected first, pointing at the top of their heads before their nose stretched out to the front. Eyes became wide and glowed as their hairs spread across their bodies.

Loud popping sounds were heard as their feet broke and transformed into hind legs while their front ones dropped to the ground. At the end of their transformation, both men stood in the middle of the room as wolves.

Casey squinted her eyes when the black one leaped onto the brown who she knew was Kenneth. He jumped out of the way through, just in time to avoid Levi's attack. Kenneth attacked then, but it backfired.

Casey held her breath as the match went on, squinting at every slash and every bite. It was intense as both wolves were fairly skilled fighters, but it was obvious Levi was the stronger of the two. Kenneth was tenacious though, refusing to give up even as his blood splattered the ground.

When Levi knocked Kenneth off his feet and leaped in the air, Casey closed her eyes and turned her head. She knew Kenneth couldn't take much more.

Seeing nothing but darkness, Casey listened as the crowd gasped, then they cheered loudly, signaling the end of the fight. She took a deep breath and held it, reluctant to open to the light, but when she did, her eyes widened and her heart drummed in her chest. Levi was lying on the ground, his tongue sticking out of his mouth and his stomach rising and dropping. Kenneth was above him, with his head to the sky, howling in victory.

Chapter 9

Casey held Kenneth around the waist, his hand around her shoulder as she helped him into his room. He was very weak and blood ran down his face and hands, but he was alive. They were both alive and safe, thanks to him.

When she helped him onto the bed, he moaned and closed his eyes. "Tell me what to do?" Casey's eyes were wild as she scanned her lover's body. He was badly wounded, but the cuts had already begun to heal.

"I'm going to need a washcloth," he said. "And time." But Kenneth had a smile on his face.

Casey chuckled, remembering the night before when he had requested the same thing. "Is that all you need?"

Kenneth smirked, and she was happy to see that he was able to lighten the situation. It meant that he was not critical. "The other thing I already have."

Though she knew his answer would be a strange remark, Casey asked, "What is that?"

Kenneth held her hand and pulled her down to him. "You."

Casey gave him a friendly smack on the shoulder and pushed herself standing again. "Well, if you have this much energy, you can make your way to the bathroom. Go have a bathe," she instructed. "The blood is bothering me."

Then there was that smirk again. "Only if you join me."

"I am not the filthy one." Casey tilted her head and pushed up her eyebrows.

She should have backed away before Kenneth took his hand and rubbed it all over her. "Now you are."

She eyed him crossly, but there was a playful smile on her lips. "Fine," she told him, pulling him from the bed. "We can both take a bath."

Kenneth's expression was one of being proud. He engulfed Casey in his arms and led her to the bathroom.

The water was warm and refreshingly sprayed the couple. Kenneth wrapped Casey in his arms and placed a kiss on his forehead. "I know I haven't been in your life long, but I don't know what I would do without you, Casey. You give my life meaning." Then he looked into her eyes, his words soft and filled with emotions. "I love you."

Casey's eyes were bright. It might have been the spray from the shower, but they were filled with moisture too. She smiled wildly and looped her hand around Kenneth's neck. "My life was definitely less eventful without you. But it was also more lonely." She pressed her body against him, her wet breast sliding on his toned chest, sending sensations throughout her body. "I love you too."

Their lips met under the stream of water as their kiss intensified. Then Kenneth turned her around and pinned her against the wall so that he faced her back. Casey's hand took purchase on the wall as her lover bent her over and passed his hand on her ass before smacking it. Casey felt his penis on her entrance then, hard and ready to enter her, but it didn't.

She groaned. "What are you waiting for?"

"I want to hear you say it. Tell me you want me," Kenneth passed his hand on her ass again before settling it on her waist.

"I want you, Kenneth. I want you much. I can't take it anymore. Take me now." Casey had barely finished her sentence when she felt his intrusion. His cock was warm and welcomed as it slid along the walls of her vagina. She moaned and pushed herself backward, sending more of him inside her. She only stopped at the shaft.

"So impatient," Kenneth said with a chuckle but began to incite her with a forceful thrust. Casey moaned with each one, clinging to the wet surface of the tiles. She pushed her ass backward every time Kenneth eased away from her, always needing to feel him inside. Her intensity that built throughout the entire act was breathtakingly passionate. When the surge finally took over her body, she fisted her hands and released a passionate moan. Kenneth wasn't finished, though. He went a few more rounds before finally releasing himself.

When they were finished, the two made their way to the bedroom. Kenneth gave Casey a t-shirt that fit her like a dress so she could wash the outfit she had. They were about to enter the kitchen to prepare a meal together when they heard a commotion in the lobby.

"Stay here," Kenneth said with his eyes narrowed and forehead creased. "I'm going to check it out."

Casey nodded, but as soon as he moved away, she took a step behind him. Kenneth walked out into the hallway and to the lobby, then suddenly stopped. Casey bumped into his back and when she peered her head to the side to see beyond his frame, her eyes widened. The lobby was filled with well-built men, each one sexier than the next, but none matching Kenneth. She recognized some of them from the fight. Two were Levi's minions.

"You've proved yourself the strongest in our clan and you were always a good leader," a blond man with blue eyes came forward. "We come to you today requesting that we join your clan. We all want to follow you."

Casey came to his side then, and his fingers laced through hers with a smile. Then he turned to the men who made the lobby seem smaller than it actually was. "Together, we would become the strongest clan."

The men erupted in cheers and hoots.

THE END